Come on,
TIGER TOM

For Lara, Mike and Vicki.
This book belongs to them – G.A.

SIMON AND SCHUSTER

First published in Great Britain in 2016 by Simon and Schuster UK Ltd

1st Floor, 222 Gray's Inn Road, London WC1X 8HB

A CBS Company · Text and illustrations copyright © 2016 Gabriel Alborozo

The right of Gabriel Alborozo to be identified as the author and illustrator of this work has

been asserted by him in accordance with the Copyright, Designs and Patents Act, 1988

All rights reserved, including the right of reproduction in whole or in part in any form

A CIP catalogue record for this book is available from the British Library upon request

ISBN: 978-1-4711-4385-4 (HB) · ISBN: 978-1-4711-4386-1 (PB) · ISBN: 978-1-4711-4387-8 (eBook)

Printed in China

1 3 5 7 9 10 8 6 4 2

Come on,
TIGER TOM

GABRIEL ALBOROZO

SIMON AND SCHUSTER
London New York Sydney Toronto New Delhi

One long, hot summer's day,
Tiger Tom and his mum went out for a walk.

Flick, flick, flick! "Got you!" said Tom,
batting the end of Mum's tail.

"Come on," said Mum, laughing.
"That's enough of that. It's time to go fishing
and I want you to watch, listen
and try your best."

They soon reached the river, and after they had cooled their paws
in the shimmery shallows, it was time for fishing practice.

"Wait for the fish then swoop with your paw like this,"
Mum whispered. "And remember, keep very, very quiet.
You need to catch the fish by surprise."

Tom tried. For a while.

But he soon wanted to play with the fish rather than catch them
and his splashing got louder and louder.

"Come on, Tiger Tom," said Mum.
"That's enough of that."

They walked a little further
and came to a gnarly old tree.

"Up you come," said Mum.
"And remember,
one paw at a time —
and don't look down!"

Tom tried. For a while.

But he soon wanted to play
with the birds perching on the tree's
branches rather than climb.

And then he looked down.

Bump!

He landed on the ground with a soft thud.

"Come on, Tiger Tom," said Mum,
after checking her little cub was all right.
"That's enough of that for today."

Tom and Mum walked on in the hot sun.

At last they reached the shadowy cool of the forest's edge,
where golden leaves lay heaped in little piles.

"This will be fun," said Mum.
"We can practise your pouncing.
Now watch. Crouch down low, like this,
and keep as still as a statue.

Then —

POW!

Out you come!"

Tom tried.
He was quite good at this.
He pounced at a red beetle.

And at a row of marching ants.

And then he pounced at a beautiful bright blue butterfly!
The butterfly flittered and fluttered through the dappled light of the forest.

Tom followed, entranced.

Flitter-flutter-flit
they went until...

...the butterfly fluttered behind a tree.

Tom peeped round it and then he looked up, down and behind it too.

But the butterfly had gone.

And Tom soon realised that he had walked deep into the forest.

It was dark and chilly. He shivered.
He turned around and around
but no matter where he looked,
he couldn't see Mum.

He was lost!

Just as Tom thought he might begin to cry,
he noticed a little chameleon scuttling
speedily up a tree.
"Aha," he thought. "If I climb
up there, I'll be able
to see Mum!"

So carefully,
one paw at a
time, he slowly
climbed the tree.

And he didn't
look down.

Tom curled himself
tightly around a high branch
and inched his way out until he
could see across the forest.

He couldn't see Mum.
But he could see the river.
Tom scrambled quickly back down the tree trunk.
If he could just get back to the river he'd find Mum for sure.

He trotted back through the trees, trying not to look at the pretty fireflies flickering in the twilight, or at the lime-green frogs hopping amongst the leaves.

This time,
he kept straight on.

By the time he reached the river,
the sky had turned inky dark
and the moon shone on the water,
silver and white.

But Tom still couldn't see Mum.

And then...

...he heard a noise.

Tom was scared.

Then he remembered what Mum
had said. *'Crouch down low
and keep as still as a statue.'*
So Tom tucked himself into a ball
and got ready to pounce.

The noise grew louder
and footsteps crunched closer
and closer towards him.

And then…

"Tom – is that you?" called a familiar voice.

And out pounced Tom **POW!**

a roly-poly bundle of pure happiness,
into a great big hug with Mum.

Phew!

The next morning, Tom woke early.
"Come on, Mum," he said, flicking
her tail gently to and fro.
"Time for fishing practice!

And this time I'm going
to do it just like you told me!"

Tom and Mum set out for the river.
And Tom watched, listened
and tried his best...

...most of the time.